THE SHIELD
OF
NIKE

A WAR ON
THE GODS
COMPANION
STORY

Cover by Gabrielle Ragusi
Interior book design by
Cloud Kitten Publishing
Edited by Nikki Mentges at
NAM Editorial

THE SHIELD
OF
NIKE

For my parents, Amy and Scott, and for my brothers, Matthew and Troy.

Without your love I may not have been able to persevere last year, and I may not have still been here to publish **The Helm of Darkness** *and to continue pursuing my writing career.*

And for Tory.

The influence you had on this story is monumental; thank you for all your help and support.

You have no idea how much it means to me.

CHAPTER ONE
VOICE

November 15th, 2018

One of the last things Greg said to Valeria before the world ended was, "Val, I'm in love with you."

The pair had been hiking that afternoon, since they'd been released from school early—they hiked any time the weather was nice enough for it and they weren't in class or at some other extracurricular activity. They'd chosen a spot overlooking a canyon of boulders, trees, and bodies of water several miles outside their little town in South Dakota.

After about an hour they'd been ready to head into town and grab some hot cocoa and a bite to eat, and were walking back to Greg's car when he'd decided to drop the bomb on Valeria about how he felt. Gray clouds filled the sky. The crisp air smelled of pine and fallen leaves.

"Val, did you hear me? I'm in love with you," he said, running a hand through his shaggy blond hair, his brown eyes fearful. He stood at the bottom of a wooden ladder pushed against a rock formation which led to the top of the hiking spot. He always made sure it was safe to climb before having Valeria go up or down it. "It's fine if you don't feel the same. But say something at least."

Valeria looked down at him, breath caught in her throat. Greg had been her best friend for years, despite their different personalities. Greg was a popular jock. He befriended all to some extent and was in every sport Valeria could think of. He performed well in most of them, while she avoided people and sports in general. She preferred to draw cartoon characters and read superhero and other various comics and graphic novels in her spare time. It irritated her father, who insisted she'd excel in athletic activities, but she'd never been interested in doing more than watch Greg play.

Now Valeria and Greg were seniors in high school, and next year they'd be off to college on opposite sides of the United States. She was going to the West Coast for art school so she could become an illustrator, and he had a few athletic-related scholarships available to him, all on the East Coast. So what if she was in love with him? So what if she always had been? In a year they'd be separated. And as gorgeous and athletic as Greg was, he'd surely find someone else in college to catch his interest. Someone perfect and beautiful, Valeria imagined.

Not that Valeria *wasn't* attractive—she knew she was. She was tall, about Greg's height, and thin, with dark eyes, ivory skin, and silky black hair. But there were lots of pretty girls, she wasn't the only one, and if she and Greg were thousands of miles apart . . .

Valeria gulped. She opened her mouth to reply; with what, she wasn't sure. But before she could utter a word, the ground trembled slightly, and she stumbled backward. "Whoa, what the—" As fast as the ground had begun to shake, it went still. Thunder *crack*ed in the distance, and the sky darkened. Raindrops showered the canyon.

The pair locked eyes. "We should hurry and get to the car before it gets worse out," Greg said, his expression crestfallen. "I didn't think we'd be caught in a storm. Forget about dinner. I'll take you home." He turned from her and started walking back.

Valeria pushed her hair behind her ears and climbed down the ladder. "Greg . . . there's something I—" She reached the ground and was cut off as it trembled again, this time more violently. She and Greg both stumbled into the grass, the ladder crashing onto its side, thunder roaring above their heads. The rain poured down harder now.

"What the hell?" Greg yelled, the ground still jolting beneath them.

"Has there ever been an earthquake in town?"

"I don't think so."

They scrambled to their feet. Greg offered his hand to Valeria. She took it without hesitation, and they sprinted along the tremoring path toward the car, flashes of lightning illuminating the sky. Within moments Valeria was drenched, sweaty, and shivering all at the same time.

After what felt like an eternity of running, Valeria spotted the road ahead of them. She thought she'd feel relief when they got there, but at the sight of it, dread flooded her body. Greg's black BMW had been parked on the

other side of the lane, but now it lay on its side. Deep cracks from the earthquake were left in the asphalt. The pair stopped in their tracks, and Greg cursed.

Valeria dropped Greg's hand and whipped out her cell phone. She tried to call her dad, but it wouldn't go through. She dialed 9-1-1, but again, the call wouldn't go through. She stuffed the phone back into her pocket. "I can't get service. Try yours."

"I left it at home."

"What are we supposed to do?"

As if to answer her, another angry *crack* of thunder sounded in the air, and from the storm clouds, three skinny golden objects soared straight for them.

Greg shoved Valeria to the side. "Look out!"

Valeria splashed into a puddle of rain and mud. The sickening sound of something sharp piercing human flesh filled her ears, and

Greg screamed. Valeria scrambled to her hands and knees and turned toward him. When she saw him, she didn't have time to wonder what was going on, or why. Because the scene before her made time stop.

On either side of Greg, what looked like two shimmering golden arrows had sunk into the ground. A third had pierced Greg through the stomach, the arrowhead poking out from his back. He lay on his side, his expression twisted in anguish. Blood already stained his white T-shirt.

Valeria's chest grew tight. The arrows had been coming toward *her*. He'd taken the blow for her. "*Greg!*" She crawled to his side and seized his hands. "What should I do?" She blinked back tears. "You're hurt . . ."

Greg squeezed her hands in his. "I d-don't know, Val." He grunted, shifting his legs as though trying to stand, then dropped them. "I can't get up."

Valeria thought of the day she and Greg met, and the tears she'd tried to hold back streamed down her face. She remembered it so clearly: at the time she'd been a seventh grader, new to the school. She'd been sitting alone at lunch that day, about to cry because she'd had to leave all her friends behind in Colorado and she had no one. But then Greg had approached her.

"You look lonely," he'd said. *"Why don't you come sit with me and my friends?"*

She remembered nodding, a little numb from shock. He'd taken her hand, then led her to his table with all his closest friends, and after a lengthy conversation about superheroes, the two had been inseparable. She went to all his games; he attended all her art shows. They took turns studying at each other's houses, and when they weren't busy with school and extracurricular activities, they hung out together with the rest of their friends.

And now an arrow was in his stomach and he was bleeding out in front of her and there was nothing she could do to help him. They were miles out of town with no cell service, and his car was turned on its side.

If Greg had just stayed put, the arrow would have hit her instead. She wished it had. What if he were to die? What would she do then? He was her best friend in the whole world. Her partner in crime. She loved him.

Valeria wept, saying Greg's name over and over, and he cupped one of her cheeks with his hand. "It's okay," he said, as though to try and comfort her, even though he was the one pierced with an arrow and bleeding to death in the mud.

Out of nowhere, a woman's voice, commanding and regal, said, *Stop crying; it will do you no good*, and Valeria jumped. The voice reverberated through her skull, as though it were coming from her own mind. But that

couldn't be. Could it?

She squinted into the rain and looked around, seeing no one. Had she lost her mind?

You are capable of so much more than you know, the woman went on. *Do not sit here and weep like a damsel locked in a tower. Save him.*

"How can I do it?" Valeria whispered, glancing at Greg. His eyes were clamped shut, his breaths shallow. Maybe she *was* crazy. But if there was a way she could save him . . .

Stand up. Go to the car. Push it upright.

Valeria furrowed her brow. "How? How in the world am I supposed to do that?" She'd never been a weakling, but it was physically impossible for her to move a car. She wasn't anything like the gifted heroes she read about in comic books. Right?

Just do it, the woman said. *Prove yourself worthy.*

Valeria wasn't sure what the woman meant by that, let alone what was going on, but she had no time to waste. The least she could do was try. She let go of Greg's hands and stood, then made her way across the street, dodging its destruction, to the black BMW.

The rain fell in massive sheets. The ground hadn't stopped tremoring. Every inch of Valeria was soaked, and she shivered from both the cold and her own fear. She squatted, placed her hands under the car's side, and, using all her might, tried to lift it upright. Just as she'd suspected, nothing happened.

Focus your energy, the woman said. *Focus it.*

Valeria grunted. "Yeah, pretty sure that's what I've been doing. It isn't going to budge."

She pulled away from the car, ready to turn back to Greg and try something else, but the woman continued, *No. You aren't focusing properly. What will save him can be found at the core of your being.*

"This is crazy," Valeria snapped. "You're

crazy. Or maybe it's me who's crazy. Since I'm the one imagining your voice and all."

If you think I am a part of your imagination, you truly are hopeless. The woman almost sounded sad. *Hopeless and weak.*

Valeria clenched her fists. "I'm not weak. You're the one asking me to do the impossible."

What I ask from you is not impossible if you would just try. But it seems you cannot. So you are weak.

Valeria shrieked in contempt and threw her hands under the car. *What will save him can be found at the core of your being,* the woman had said. *Focus your energy.* Valeria closed her eyes and imagined herself as a hero like Hulk, Thor, or Wonder Woman. She imagined herself as someone with super-strength who could lift a car with ease.

You have to save Greg, she thought, the image of an arrow in his stomach flashing across her mind. *This is crazy. But you're doing it for him.*

Valeria gasped and opened her eyes as a flood of pulsing hot energy burst from the center of her chest and shot through her arms. She looked to the hunk of metal under her palms and focused the energy into them, then pushed up. Every muscle in her body tingled and burned. It felt as if the sparks of a firecracker danced along them. She cried out and gritted her teeth, putting all her strength into the task at hand.

With a loud *creeeeeeaaaak*, she pushed the BMW onto its wheels.

Marvelous, said the woman. *You have begun your journey, my child. You have proven yourself worthy.*

Valeria stumbled backward, staring wide-eyed at the car. "No freaking way." She had so many questions to ask the disembodied woman, her mind racing with confusion at the events that had just transpired. But there was no time.

Greg was still in trouble.

Valeria spun around and dashed toward Greg. She had to carry him to the car, drive back into town, and take him to the emergency room. But just as she reached his side, something hard collided with the back of her head.

Her senses grew fuzzy and she swayed to the side. She stumbled into the mud, then fell insensible.

Valeria's head throbbed with pain, and she opened her eyes. They felt heavy, like when she'd stayed up all night and only gotten a few hours of sleep before she needed to be at school. Her vision spun the walls of her room into a twisted mess of dull gray, orange, red, and yellow. Good thing she didn't have class today; she could curl into a ball and go back to bed. She'd sleep and let this headache pass.

Something was wrong, though. Her clothes and hair were cool and damp, as though she'd taken a dip in a lake fully clothed hours before and never dried off. Not only that, but she had no blankets and no pillow, and her mattress didn't feel anything like a mattress. It felt more like mud and crunchy leaves.

I didn't go to bed, she remembered. *I was hiking with Greg and then . . .*

The events from earlier that day came flooding back to her.

Valeria shot up, frantically scanning the area for her friend, the scenery around her swaying back and forth like a kid on a swing. Where he once lay, only a bloody golden arrow and streaks of scarlet remained in the wet grass. Nausea bubbled in her gut.

Where could he have gone? Why had he left her there, all alone, after he'd basically sacrificed his life for hers? What in the world was going on?

Valeria stumbled forward and clung to the branches of a tree rooted beside her. "Greg," she croaked, her eyes filling with tears. "Greg . . ."

Cease your sniveling, the woman's voice said in Valeria's head. *This is not the time.*

Valeria wiped her eyes with the sleeve of her filthy purple sweatshirt. "What's—going—on?" She glared at the overcast sky. "Who are you? What do you want from me?"

For a while, the voice said nothing, and Valeria held tight to the tree, taking deep, slow breaths. Finally, her stomach settled, and the canyon stopped swaying. Its rich fall colors were more muted now, as though the leaves and grass and sky had all been dipped in a not-fully-opaque gray paint. It wasn't raining anymore, and the earthquake had stopped. Fog crawled along the ground.

Valeria shivered—the sight of the canyon was totally creepy—then looked to see if the BMW was gone. It still sat on the road where she'd pushed it upright. Dents and scratches covered the side it had fallen on, but it was intact nonetheless.

Where had Greg gone? His car was here, but he wasn't. She needed to call him. If not him, she needed to call his parents or one of his sisters. And if they hadn't seen him, she'd call the police to report him missing. Surely now that the storm was over she'd have a signal again. She pulled out her cell phone and tried to call Greg. It wouldn't go through.

Valeria sighed in exasperation and made her way toward Greg's car. Was there a way she could break into it and start it up without the keys? She'd never done anything like that before, but surely she could figure something out.

She peered into the driver-side window and spotted Greg's keys in the ignition, then furrowed her brow and tugged on the door. To her surprise, it opened with ease.

Why would he leave his car unlocked with the keys in it? she wondered. *And how did he even get to the car? He had an arrow in his stomach. This doesn't make any sense.*

He did not leave you by his own free will, the woman responded, as though she'd read

Valeria's mind. *He was taken from here, but he is safe. For now.*

Valeria swung around, her hands clenched. "Who are you? What have you done with Greg? Give him back!"

I do not have him.

"Where is he?"

Back in your town. Perhaps you should go look for him?

Valeria hurried into the driver's seat and started the engine.

Before you go, know this, the woman continued. *If you leave here without the shield, you will surely perish.*

Valeria rolled her eyes. "What are you talking about *now*? What shield? There is no shield."

The shield that fell from the sky. It hit you in the head, and you were knocked unconscious. Take it with you, my child.

Valeria stepped out of the car and looked

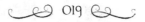

around. Sure enough, a shield the size of a small car tire lay in the grass. The fog moved around it, as though it were encased in an invisible force-field. It was a shiny, reflective orange-gold, with a laurel wreath carved into it. The sight of it creeped Valeria out more than the weird storm and the arrows that seemingly came from the sky.

Valeria gestured toward the shield. "You think taking this is the only way I'll survive?"

It is ultimately your choice whether you allow the shield to aid you on your journey, the woman replied. *But if you do not take it, and if you do not use the gifts given to you at birth, I am sure you will die.*

"Wait, wait, wait," Valeria cried, throwing her hands in the air. "Gifts given to me at birth? When did that come into the equation? And what the hell do you mean? Lady, this is getting weirder by the second."

You already know of one gift. It is the

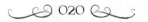

strength you possess, although it can only be accessed if you tap into it. Why do you think you were able to push the car upright?

Valeria paused. That fact was odd, yes, but she'd been too concerned about Greg to ask how she'd been able to do it.

In time, you will discover the other gift if you focus your energy. That is all I can say.

Questions swarmed Valeria's mind. Why did she need the shield to survive going home? What could have possibly happened there for that to be the reality? The woman hadn't said anything about Valeria's father, either. Was he okay? And what about her gifts? One of them seemed to be super-strength, almost like a comic book superhero's, but where did the gifts come from? Who'd given them to her?

Only one thing was certain. The woman said Greg was in town, and that he was only safe "for now." Valeria had to find him and save him before something worse happened.

She picked up the shield. She thought it would weigh a ton, but it was lighter than expected. On the inner side of the shield, what looked like hundreds of words in another language had been carved. Even more surprising than all that, it warmed her hands, as if it were radiating a heat of its own.

She climbed into the car, shoved the shield into the passenger seat, and started driving back.

CHAPTER THREE
TOWN

Valeria's hands trembled as she gripped the steering wheel. The fog was even thicker in town, but it wasn't thick enough to hide the corpses. She'd never seen so many dead bodies in her life.

In fact, the only dead person she'd ever seen was her grandfather after he'd died of a heart attack when she was nine. She'd been heartbroken over it, of course, but her father had been even more devastated. Her grandfather was the only family her father had had left, besides her, his only child.

But out of everything she remembered from that experience, what stood out the most was how her grandfather hadn't looked quite right. He'd looked less like himself and more like a pale, waxy figurine. It had taken everything in her not to scream when she'd seen him.

As she drove back into town, the dead bodies scattered around reminded her of what her grandfather had looked like in death: terrifying. Except it was clear none of them had died of a heart attack. It seemed as though the strange storm had been worse here, and she guessed, with a paralyzing rush of fear, it had killed everyone she came across.

Whole buildings were toppled over, limbs sticking out from the debris. *Probably from the earthquake*, she thought. Gold and silver arrows littered the ground, and many had pierced and killed people, their frozen faces twisted in terror. Some bodies lay, charred completely black, in smoking craters along the cracked roads, sidewalks, and parking lots, as if they'd been struck by lightning bolts on steroids. Hundreds of vehicles had crashed into each other.

Valeria's breaths came in panicked gasps now. She was pretty sure Greg was still alive—that's what the voice said at least—but what about her father? If all these people hadn't made it . . .

As if reading her thoughts again, the woman spoke in her head. *Do not go home. You will be wasting your time. You must find your friend before it is too late.*

"What about my dad?" Valeria asked, a knot in her throat. She could handle what she'd seen today thus far, although it was difficult, but if her father hadn't survived . . . "Is my dad okay?" The woman didn't reply, and dread overcame Valeria. She sped toward her house, dodging the bodies and wreckage.

Within a couple of minutes, and after spotting hundreds more people dead, she reached her neighborhood. What were once beautiful homes had been reduced to piles of brick, stucco,

wood, and glass.

She recalled when she and her father had first moved here. She'd been shocked to see how nice the houses were. Most were huge, at least two stories tall, and looked pretty much brand new.

"Don't some of these remind you of castles, Val?" her father had asked, a proud grin on his face as they'd driven down the street.

She remembered pouting in the passenger seat, arms crossed, refusing to admit how impressed she really was with their new neighborhood. She hadn't wanted to move there; she'd wanted to stay in Denver. But her father's business had grown, and he'd needed to move so he could work closer with a couple of the new restaurants he'd opened in South Dakota.

As upset as she had been in that moment, she wished she could go back to it now.

When Valeria finally reached her house, she was surprised to find it still standing. The only damage it looked as though it had suffered was that the wide entryway doors were knocked in. She slammed her foot down on the brake. The car came to a halt, and she clambered out the driver door.

Do not forget the shield! the woman reminded her. *You need it here!*

But Valeria couldn't waste even a second. She dashed up the driveway; she *needed* to find out if her father was okay. Besides, she didn't think the shield was as important as the woman made it out to be, and there was nothing around that could hurt her. Scare the crap out of her probably, but not hurt her.

She burst into the house, fog curling in from outside. The entryway, living room, and dining area were in disarray. The carpet and rugs were shredded, as though large claws had ripped them apart, and the couch, chairs, and tables were all turned on their sides and scattered about. Drawings she'd done, ones her

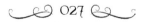

father had framed after they'd come home from art shows, had fallen off the walls, chunks of broken glass from their frames strewn across the floor.

"Dad?" Valeria called, her heart racing. "Dad, where are you?" No response.

She ran up the stairs to the second level of the house, where both of their bedrooms resided. Up here looked fine, except many of their belongings were on the floor.

It is not safe here, the woman said. *But if you leave now, you will still have time to escape Orth—*

"Would you shut up already?" Valeria snapped, her eyes burning as she held back tears. Regardless of whether or not the voice was helping her, she really, *really* wanted it to shut its trap. "Unless you wanna tell me where my dad is, and whether or not he's okay, then don't talk to me." The woman said nothing, and Valeria sniffled, wiping her eyes.

After doing a quick search of the upstairs and finding no sign of her father, she hurried back down the stairs, then through the hall toward his office on the other side of the house.

When she reached the end of the hall, she noticed the door to his office had been knocked in like the entryway doors. She jumped over it and rushed into the room. The sliding glass doors leading to the deck overlooking their backyard were shattered, and fog crept toward her feet from outside. Her father's folders and documents were strewn about the floor. The wooden case he stored his guns in had been left open.

Over the years, Valeria had gone hunting several times with her father, and he'd taught her quite a bit about guns and how to use them. She peeked into the case; his Ithaca 12-gauge pump shotgun was missing.

What the hell happened? she thought, walking out the shattered office doors onto the

deck. Glass *crunch*ed under her sneakers.

When she made it outside and caught sight of the scene taking place on her fog-infested lawn, she wished she'd listened to the voice in her head and never come back to her house.

Twenty feet ahead of her stood a black wolf-dog the size of a horse, with a writhing snake for a tail and claws longer than steak knives, its back turned to her. Blood was splattered across the grass. Her dad's shotgun lay near the dog's paws.

Its snake tail hissed at her, and the dog swung around. Instead of one head it had two, complete with glowing red eyes. Both of its mouths were lined with rows of sharklike teeth, what appeared to be human entrails stuck between them like soggy bites of spaghetti dripping with tomato sauce.

Valeria gasped and backed up toward the office. "Lady, what is that *thing*? Did it hurt my dad?"

Before the woman in her head could respond, the dog's heads made choking noises. One head spit out chewed pieces of bones, some bodily tissues still attached, while the other coughed up a tattered blue polo shirt stained with blood and guts. Valeria recognized it as one of a few Christmas presents she'd gotten her father the year before. Her stomach twisted tight as the realization hit.

I am truly sorry, the woman said, her voice cracking as though she were about to cry. *I tried to protect him, and I was able to keep the house safe from lightning and from collapsing during the earthquake. But I could not stop what happened next. I had to protect you from them.*

Valeria's eyes filled with fresh tears. Her father was the only family she'd had left. He had been a hard-working man, born in South Korea. He'd immigrated to the United States as a child with his parents and, when he turned twenty-one, started his own restaurant chain.

Valeria's mother had abandoned him when she was just a baby, but he hadn't let that get him down. He'd given Valeria the kind of life other kids dreamed of.

The two-headed dog narrowed its eyes at Valeria, and both heads howled. Chills ran through her body.

You must go, the woman cried. *Get the shield! Use your gifts!*

Valeria needed answers. Where had this weird creature come from? Who were these people the woman said she had to protect Valeria from? Were they the cause of the freak storm? The cause of all the deaths of the people in her town?

What was going on?

The monster ran toward her, the ground tremoring each time one of its paws hit the lawn. There wasn't time to ask any more questions. She raced back inside, then dashed down the hall and out the entryway.

Behind her, the monster's howls and pounding footsteps shook the house.

Valeria's heart pounded as she darted down the driveway toward Greg's car, the dog-monster just inches from biting off her head.

Your gifts, the woman said, over and over. *Use your gifts!* So far, all Valeria knew of her "gifts" was the super-strength she'd only been able to use once. And if her father hadn't stood a chance against this thing with a 12-gauge shotgun, what good would a little extra strength do her? She needed to escape; there was no way she could kill the monster.

Valeria reached the car and threw open the door, then jumped inside and rammed the keys into the ignition. The monster slammed a paw onto the roof of the car. Its claws tore through the metal, almost piercing her, and she screamed.

You must slay Orthrus, the woman said. *There is no other way. You cannot escape him. Wherever you go, he will follow, unless he is dead. And you will run out of energy before he does.*

"Oh, so this thing has a name now?" Valeria asked as Orthrus thrust another paw onto the car and sent his claws through the roof. "And how in the hell do you expect me to 'slay' him? My dad couldn't even take him out with a *gun*!"

The woman continued, *Orthrus cannot be killed with modern weapons such as "guns." Only with ancient ones such as your gifts, the shield, and . . . this.*

Golden light flashed before Valeria, and a sleek, foot-long orange-gold dagger with a wooden handle appeared, spinning in midair inches from her face. Under normal circum-

stances, she would have freaked out if a knife appeared out of nowhere in front of her, but these weren't exactly normal circumstances, and at this point she'd seen crazier.

Use these, and perhaps you can defeat him. If you survive, I will give you the answers you seek regarding what has happened to your town, and where to find your friend. Now go, slay the beast!

"At least we can agree he isn't exactly a household pet," Valeria replied, grabbing both the dagger and the shield and scrambling out the passenger door, darting beneath Orthrus's claws. She somersaulted into the street, then slipped one arm through the leather straps of the shield and secured it. Orthrus snarled and ripped his paws from the car. In one swift movement, he leapt over the BMW and landed a few feet in front of her.

If killing this thing was the only way to survive, and the only way to get answers out of the woman talking in Valeria's head . . . well, what choice did she have other than to fight it?

"Okay, I've got the shield and the knife—now what do I do?" Valeria asked. Orthrus advanced on her. She leapt to the side. His heads banged into the BMW.

Use your strength, the woman answered. *Your speed. Focus your power. Prove your worth to me a second time.*

The monster turned toward Valeria and snarled. She held up the shield, tightening her grip on the dagger and focusing her strength.

A familiar flood of pulsing hot energy burst from her chest and traveled through her arms, the muscles in her body tingling and burning. Orthrus lunged for her, and when he got close enough, using all her might, she rammed the shield into him. It *crack*ed against one of his skulls. She swiped the dagger at him. It sliced his cheek. He fell back, howling.

All at once Valeria felt more capable of fending for herself. She felt almost . . . *powerful.*

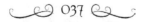

She felt maybe, just maybe, she could be like the superheroes she read about in comics. Perhaps the woman was right. Perhaps if she used the weapons and her gifts, she had a chance to survive this.

She turned toward Orthrus. Gooey moss-green liquid trickled down his cheek. He growled, dragging his feet across the sidewalk. His claws left long gouges in the concrete. Her heart still raced, and her palms were sweating, but despite her fear, a new sense of determination spread through her.

Orthrus bounded toward her, then raised a paw above her head. She threw up the shield, concentrating her strength, and his paw struck it. Sparks arced across its metal. Valeria stumbled backward. Orthrus snarled, shoving harder against her, but his claws couldn't penetrate the shield.

Excellent, the woman said. *Now your speed. Use your speed to get away from him!*

Valeria swallowed hard and focused on the energy in her body. She imagined it growing stronger in her heart, lungs, and legs, still pushing the shield back against Orthrus. He pulled away, then snapped one pair of jaws at her sneakers. She dodged the attack and darted around him. As she ran, the neighborhood around her blurred, her feet racing her away at an unimaginable pace.

When she stopped only a second later, she stood hundreds of feet away from the monster. "Holy shit!" she cried. When the woman in her head said "use your speed," she wasn't kidding. Super-speed must have been Valeria's other gift.

Orthrus bared his teeth and pounded toward her. She stood her ground, readying her weapons again. The monster reached her and reared back on his hind legs. She leapt into the air and, channeling speed into her hand movements, sliced his chest with the dagger once, twice. He howled in pain, then slammed

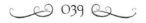

himself into the shield. She crashed into the road, losing grip of the knife. It slid out of reach.

The monster's heads snarled in Valeria's face, spit spraying from his mouths. The stench of death hung on his saliva. She pushed up with the shield, trying to tap into her strength, trying to get him off. He pressed harder. It felt as though he were crushing her ribs. She gasped for breath.

Do not give up now, the woman said. *Focus your power!* But Valeria couldn't do that; her vision spun.

She imagined the terror her father must have felt in his last moments, and tears trickled down her temples onto the asphalt. It finally hit her: she'd never see her father again. Never give him a hug as he came home from work. He'd never see her graduate, never walk her down the aisle on her wedding day. Never meet his grandchildren.

Would it be so bad to die? She believed

in life after death, and so did her father. If she died, wouldn't she see him again? She could let Orthrus win . . .

But then she imagined how Greg must feel right now. All alone, with everyone else in town dead, probably being chased by some monster of his own. Probably wondering, *Where's Val? Is she okay?* And here she was, getting squished by a huge two-headed dog and the shield she'd been using to fight it.

"*Val, I'm in love with you,*" Greg had said, right before their whole world shattered.

I'm in love with you too, she thought. *I wish I'd been brave enough to tell you that when I had the chance. I wish I could tell you now.*

The woman interjected on her thoughts, *You could tell your friend you love him if you would just fight. He is still alive, and he needs your help.*

The woman was right. Valeria couldn't let Orthrus win; she couldn't die. Not now.

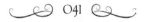

Not while Greg was still out there. Not while he still needed her.

She gritted her teeth and willed her muscles to ignite with power. She imagined herself as a superhero with strength powerful enough to push this ugly-ass dog off her. And she imagined she could slay it afterward.

Within moments, fiery energy burst from her chest and raced through her limbs. Using all her might, she shoved the shield upward, and Orthrus went flying backward. He collided with the road thirty feet away.

Valeria hopped to her feet. She seized the dagger and concentrated on her gifts: on her strength, on her speed. She advanced on Orthrus, blade held high above her head. Her surroundings blurred. In a quarter of a second she jumped onto his back.

The monster's serpent tail lunged at her. His heads bent over backward to gnash their jaws at her. She dodged the attacks, using the strength in her legs to leap high into the air. As she soared back down, she shoved the dagger into the base of his neck, then, with a satisfying *cruuuunch*, tore it through the rest of his back.

Orthrus let out a long howl, his serpent tail screaming, then collapsed in the street. Green fluid pooled around his body.

Valeria climbed off his back and stood for a while, unable to believe that she not only had superpowers, but also had killed a freaky two-headed dog with a snake for its tail. As she caught her breath, an odd burning sensation spread through her chest. "I must be more out of shape than I thought," she wheezed.

Once she'd gathered her composure for the most part, she recalled what the woman in her head had said about telling her what was going on.

Valeria waved the knife at the sky. "Okay, lady. I'm ready for some freaking answers." She gestured toward Orthrus's body. "You said you'd

tell me what's going on and where to find Greg if I defeated this guy. Well, here you go. He's defeated."

For a moment, the woman didn't answer, and Valeria wondered if this was a nightmare. Maybe she'd wake up any second now and find her father and everyone in her town still alive, Greg safe at home with his family.

She closed her eyes, praying for that to be the truth, until the woman said, *Yes, my child. You have proven yourself worthy of my guidance a second time. I will give you the answers you seek. But first, allow me to introduce myself.*

Brilliant light flashed before Valeria's eyes.

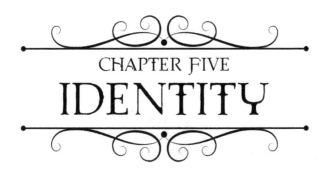

CHAPTER FIVE
IDENTITY

When the light finally faded, a pretty woman dressed in deep-purple robes stood before her in the middle of the road. Over a foot taller than Valeria, she was lean and tan, with hazel eyes and long brown hair braided down her back. Shimmering orange-gold feathered wings stemmed from her shoulder blades, her wrists and neck adorned with matching jewelry.

Despite the woman's odd appearance and the fact Valeria had never seen her before, something about her seemed familiar.

Before either of them could say a word, the burning sensation in Valeria's chest grew worse, and she doubled over. "What the hell—"

"Let me help," the woman said, hurrying to her side. "You must have overexerted your powers. Try not to do that often, or else you could burn up your body and kill yourself."

Valeria chuckled. "Of course I couldn't have unlimited superpowers. That'd make this too easy."

The woman smiled, resting a hand on Valeria's shoulder, and within seconds the burning sensation dulled. "I cannot fully rejuvenate you—your body will have to do that itself—but I can give you some of my strength," she said, then pulled away and bowed. "I have been waiting to reveal myself to you since you were born. My name is Nike. I am the Goddess of Strength, Speed, and Victory."

"Wait, hold on a second," Valeria said, raising her eyebrows. "First off, you said your name is *Nike*? Do you mean like the tennis shoes?"

Nike smirked. "The brand uses my name,

and they do make 'tennis shoes,' yes. They are one of the reasons I have not faded away yet."

"And you say you're a goddess? I mean, I'm pretty sure there's only one god, and I don't think that guy makes trips to earth anymore or has had any kids in the last several thousand years."

"If the particular god you speak of does exist, then he hasn't interfered with what we, the Greek gods, have done as of late."

"Greek gods? You mean like Zeus and Hades and Aphrodite? You're one of them? But—I'm pretty sure they're just myths."

Nike sighed and stepped forward. She rested a hand on Valeria's shoulder. "My child, the Greek gods, goddesses, and monsters you have been told are myths are real. You fought a monster yourself, just now: the two-headed dog, Orthrus. In the old days, he guarded Geryon's cattle and was slain by Heracles, but he was resurrected for— Well, let's just say he was brought back for a reason I cannot disclose at this time. But why do you think your father could not slay the beast with a gun, while you were able to defeat him using the weapons I gave you? It is because when the gods who resurrected Orthrus sent him to earth, they made him invincible against modern weapons. After all, the modern age is part of why the Greek gods have begun to fade away. Why allow it to rule any longer?

"The gods have been real for thousands of years, and because of what has happened, we will be real for thousands to come. I will explain more, but you did not let me finish all I meant to say before. There is more I must tell you. Something you should know; something I wish I could have told you before now."

Nike paused, and for a while it was so quiet Valeria could hear the blood pounding in her ears. She still didn't buy everything this "goddess" was saying, so why did the next piece of information matter so much? None of it sounded real anyway. But then again, she couldn't exactly come up with a better explanation for it all herself.

Finally, Nike said, "Valeria—I am your mother."

Valeria backed away. Nike couldn't be her mother, could she? "No way. You're crazy. If you're a goddess and my mom—I mean, why didn't my dad tell me? And don't say it would be hard to miss." She took a deep, shaky breath. "All my dad ever said was he met my mom at a football game in Denver, and after she got pregnant, she came to live with him until I was born. She stayed long enough to name me, and then she vanished. That's uncool. What kind of a mom does that? If you're really my mom, tell me why you did that to him. Why you did that to me."

"Because I am a goddess, and I had more pressing matters to attend to. Your father knew that. He also knew he wouldn't be able to tell you the truth about your heritage. That was something I would have to do myself. But why do you think he always wanted you to go out for sports? He knew the potential you had with your mother being a goddess of strength and speed. You could have dominated every game you played, even if you only tapped into a quarter of your abilities."

Valeria paused. Was she going insane, or was Nike starting to make sense? "All right. Say I'm your daughter. If you're really a goddess, what does that make me? Am I a goddess too? Or just a regular girl with some cool abilities?"

"You are a demigod. There have been many like you in the past, and there will be many more in the future. Demigods are half human, half god. Most are mortal, as are you, and therefore you will die one day, as all mortals do. But precious gifts from my divine power were bestowed on you upon conception: your strength and your speed."

"So I'm a regular girl with some cool abilities. I didn't need the fancy explanation, but thanks." She bit her lip. "Look, this is a lot to process. Yesterday I was just a regular teenager getting ready for art school next year. I was fine with my dad being my only family. I grew up without a mom, so I've never known any different. And within less than a day it seems like the world is ending. My dad is dead. My best friend is missing, and you said he's only safe for now. Not to mention all of a sudden I have superpowers and my mom shows up and says she's a mythical goddess named after tennis shoes. I guess what I'm trying to say is, I'm really, really confused. Could you tell me what happened to my town? And where Greg is, like you said you would?"

Nike cocked her head and narrowed her eyes as though listening for something. "They're calling me."

"What are you talking about?" Valeria asked.

Nike turned to Valeria, her body dissolving like snowflakes melting before they could land. "They say I can tell you no more. I must go."

Valeria threw her hands in the air. "But you haven't even told me what you said you would."

"I know, and I am sorry, but I cannot disobey them. Goodbye, my child." And with that, Nike disappeared altogether.

Valeria kicked the road, more frustrated than ever. Nike hadn't answered any of her questions about what had happened to her town or where Greg was, and had only generated more confusion. Her lip quivered. She was starting to think she would never find out what was going on. What if she couldn't find Greg? What if she couldn't save him? Then what?

I'll have no one, she thought. *Not Grand-*

pa. Not Dad. Not Greg. I'll be all alone, and it won't matter if I have superpowers and my mom is a goddess. Because everyone I love the most will be gone.

The distant scream of a young man pierced the air, and Valeria snapped to attention. It sounded like Greg. She called his name twice, and the cry sounded again. And again. And again.

Valeria could use her super-speed to reach who she hoped was Greg, but she didn't want to overexert her powers and kill herself, like Nike said she would if she did too much. If that happened, she definitely wouldn't find Greg. No, she'd be better off driving in the direction of the yells and getting out to look for him once she was close enough.

She ran back to the BMW, jumped inside, and tossed Nike's shield and dagger into the passenger seat. The keys were still in the ignition.

She started the engine and rolled down

the windows, then sped toward the far-away screams.

CHAPTER SIX
CORPSE

The sun began to set, bits of pink, orange, and purple cutting through the clouds and fog, and Valeria tried not to panic. Looking for Greg among the wreckage and dead bodies was scary enough, but doing so in the night sounded like a special kind of terrifying. Plus, Nike hadn't spoken to her since their meeting. It looked as if Valeria was on her own now.

The young man's cries stopped before she could pinpoint where they were coming from, so she decided to search the general areas she thought he could be and hoped he was okay. She drove through a couple of neighborhoods, and after finding nothing, parked behind what used to be two lines of shops across from each other in the center of town. She shut off the car, grabbed the shield and dagger in case she met some other freaky monster, and made her way between a couple of the collapsed buildings toward the street. "Greg?" she called. No reply but eerie silence.

Valeria walked along the road, weaving between crashed cars and cracks in the asphalt. She peered through the fog, then stopped dead, shivers crawling up her spine. There were so many corpses scattered here she couldn't count them all. She shook her head and began wandering farther, avoiding their cold, blank gazes. Yes, she had to keep going. But what if she saw someone she knew?

Don't think about that.

After a while, as the sun continued to set, she guessed she had a little less than a half hour before it got dark. She didn't want to be far from the car when that happened, so she started back toward where she'd parked. Hopefully she'd find Greg soon. She wasn't sure how much time he had left, if any at all.

When she'd almost reached the BMW, the pained moan of a girl sounded behind her.

Valeria whipped around. "Hello?" She surveyed the street, but all she saw was rubble and craters. "Is anyone there?" Another moan. Maybe being alone for so long was making her hear things?

She walked farther down the street to investigate where the noises were coming from and spotted a teenage girl limping toward her through the fog, illuminated by the glaring light of the sunset.

Valeria started for the girl. She couldn't believe she'd found another living person. Were there others? Had she overlooked them in her quest to find Greg? "Oh my God, are you okay?" The girl groaned in response. Had she not heard the question? Was she badly injured?

Valeria quickened her pace and prayed she could help in whatever way this girl needed.

When Valeria made it about ten feet away from the girl, she recognized the girl as Jennifer Hernandez, a cute cheerleader and junior in high school that Greg had dated for a few months a year or so ago. Valeria liked Jennifer. She was sweet, but Greg had said their relationship "just wasn't right". Did that have anything to do with the feelings he had for Valeria? Just thinking about it made her feel guilty; Jennifer had been pretty torn up when Greg had broken up with her. "Jennifer? Are you okay? It's me, Valeria Lee."

Jennifer groaned again, and Valeria stepped back. The more she examined Jennifer, the more something didn't seem right. Dried blood caked the girl's dark hair, her usually animated eyes dull and lifeless. Her brown skin looked pale and ashen. Her movements were stiff as she limped toward Valeria, as if she'd been left in a freezer and was trying to thaw, all her bodily fluids now slush instead of liquid.

"Hello?" Valeria called, heart in her throat.

"Uuuurrr," Jennifer replied, her mouth twitching.

Valeria continued backing away. "Hey, are you okay?"

"*Uuuuuuuuuuuuuurrrrrrrrrr.*"

"I'll take that as a no," Valeria said, and ran the other way. She had no idea what was wrong with Jennifer, but she'd read enough alien-parasite and zombie media to not stick around and find out.

More moans sounded from behind, and Valeria looked back. Jennifer still limped along, slow and steady, but now several other figures shuffled alongside her too.

Valeria's heart dropped. "Nike, what's happening?" She hoped the goddess would pop up in her head again, but there was no reply.

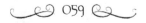

She glanced at the sky to see the sun almost below the horizon and cursed under her breath.

More people dragged themselves out from debris and wrecked cars, blocking Valeria's way. The sight of them made her skin crawl; they were covered in dried blood and guts. Some looked as if they'd been partially flattened under toppled buildings, some had arrows stuck in their bodies, and some were charred to a crisp. They reached their stiff arms out to Valeria as if trying to grab her, moaning and groaning all the while.

Were they legitimate risen corpses, like in *The Walking Dead*? It seemed plausible at this point. If Greek gods and myths were real, anything was possible, right? She wasn't completely up to date on her Greek mythology, but she couldn't recall any zombie myths.

It didn't matter. Whatever these people were, they weren't out for her best interests.

Three young men with arrows sticking

out of their abdomens shuffled faster than the others toward Valeria. She readied her weapons and, although her chest still burned from earlier, channeled her strength. Her muscles ignited with power. She stabbed one of the men between the eyes. He let out a final groan and collapsed face-first in the road.

Valeria gulped down vomit. "All right, so you're more like those guys in *The Walking Dead*. I'll take it." She raised the shield and pushed the other two back. They fell on their butts, and in two swift movements, she stabbed their brains too.

Behind her, the cackle of a teenage girl cut through the air, and Valeria turned, goose bumps rising on her arms. Jennifer and her posse of zombies still limped toward her, but Jennifer's eyes glowed bright-white now, her mouth twisted into a stiff, sinister smile.

"Jennifer? Is that you?"

"The mortal is gone, foolish demigod,"

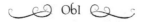

Jennifer's corpse spat. "There is only one in control of these shells now."

"Yeah? And who might that 'one' be?"

Jennifer paused. The rest of the dead people stopped along with her and swayed back and forth on their feet. Jennifer contorted her expression, scowling at Valeria. "It is I, Hades, King of the Underworld, God of the Dead and Riches. I cannot leave my domain, for Zeus has not permitted it. However, I can speak to you through my minions of death."

Valeria raised her eyebrows. She'd heard of Hades before. Maybe he'd give her more info than Nike had. "Hades, huh? What's up? How are you?"

Hades stomped Jennifer's foot. "Insolent demigod. I am not here to converse with you. I am here to destroy you."

"While you're at it, could you tell me what happened to my town? I mean, I figure you'd know, since you're kind of a big deal, being a god and all."

The god made Jennifer cackle. "What happened to the town? Oh, foul Daughter of Nike, did your mother not tell you? I thought she would. Perhaps my brothers advised her against it. I cannot fathom why they would—I think it better if you knew. But it is no matter. I will explain.

"At one time, we, the Greek gods, were all-powerful. We were unstoppable. However, as the years passed, not only did humans become more monotheistic, but their thirst for knowledge caused them to advance in technology so much they had no need for gods anymore. We were reduced to nothing more than myth. Some of us even began to fade away completely. We had to take matters into our own hands.

"We destroyed not only your town, Daughter of Nike, but also your whole world. We sent the Storm. The earthquakes, the arrows, the lightning. And now that we are here again, humanity will pay. We will take back the glory we once possessed."

Valeria swallowed hard. The gods hadn't messed with just her town, but with the whole world? She tried to imagine how many millions of people across the globe were dead. Her mind raced; this was bigger than she could have ever imagined. "Okay. You sent the freaky storm to punish people? Because they don't believe in you anymore? Are you being serious right now?"

Hades forced Jennifer to give a slow nod. "Correct. We did this to remind the humans of who we are so that we may rule the world once again."

"What about Orthrus? Did you send him to punish humanity too?"

"No."

"Okay, then why'd you send him?"

"We sent him to test you."

Valeria's nostrils flared. If it weren't for Orthrus, her dad would still be alive; Nike had protected him from everything else. And it was all because some gods wanted to "test" her? For what? And why? Were they so uncreative they couldn't think of a different way to test people? Her father's life was more important than something so stupid. Not only that, but the lives of people in general were more important than ruling the earth. These gods seemed less like all-powerful, omniscient beings, and more like toddlers fighting over a toy. "What do you mean, you sent him to test me?"

"I think that is enough questions for today," Hades said. "It is time for my minions of death to feast on your flesh while I relish in the fact that the last bit of knowledge you will have gained in your pathetic life was that we finally destroyed your world."

The glowing, bright-white light faded from Jennifer's eyes. The sun dropped below the horizon, and corpses advanced on Valeria.

She gritted her teeth. Not only was her

chest still burning, but she also didn't want to fight the zombies. She knew at one point they'd been living, breathing people; people she once walked past at the store, or saw at a busy restaurant, or went to school with. What had happened to them wasn't fair or right. Killing whatever they were now wouldn't change it. But she also knew she didn't want to be their dinner. So she concentrated on her strength, trying not to overdo it, and decided to start stabbing and/or smashing their brains.

Six of them with parts of their bodies flattened and crusted over with guts came at her. Three moaned and groaned, trying to grab her, grinding their teeth. She swiped her dagger at them, and the blade sliced through their skulls, one by one.

Using the shield, she shoved the other three to the ground. They scratched at the shield with corpse-blue hands. In several swift motions, she stabbed them between the eyes.

More zombies shuffled toward her. She continued killing them, either by using her shield to pummel their skulls into bloody pulp or by stabbing their heads. But even after it seemed as if all of them were taken care of, more showed up, stumbling toward her through the fog.

Her chest burned hotter now. It was as if flames were clawing at her rib cage, threatening to spread through her body and reduce her to ashes.

Valeria realized she needed to get away. She had no idea how many corpses Hades would send after her. For all she knew, he could send infinite amounts, and she wasn't sure she had the strength to kill even twenty more. She mowed down four standing between her and the path toward the BMW, then sprinted for the car.

Before she could reach it, the enraged cry of a young man pierced the air behind her. *Greg?* Valeria stopped, whipped around, and witnessed a sight that terrified her more than

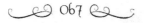

anything she'd seen yet.

Past the horde of zombies, a giant of a woman with a flaming torch in one hand crept out from behind a heap of fallen buildings. She stood at least thirty feet tall. Her eyes glowed red, her tanned skin worn and leathery, her black hair in a matted braid over her shoulder. Her wide torso rippled with muscles, tattered cloth stained with blood covering her large breasts. A belt of human skulls hung around her hips. Strangest of all, instead of legs she had the long tail of an emerald-green serpent curling far behind her.

As the woman slithered closer, Valeria noticed she held something else in her other hand. She squinted to get a better look, and her heart leapt in her chest. It looked like a squirming young man with shaggy blond hair.

"Val!" Greg screamed. "Val, *run!*"

CHAPTER SEVEN
MOTHER

The snake-woman crushed zombies beneath her tail with ease as she slithered toward Valeria.

Greg pounded his fists against the woman's fingers wrapped tight around his abdomen. "Val, did you hear me?" he cried. "Run! Get outta here!"

The truth was, Valeria *wanted* to run away. Just looking at the woman made her heart race, her palms growing slippery with sweat. But she wouldn't leave Greg. She couldn't, not in a million years. Not after he'd risked his life for her, and *especially* not when he was in the clutches of a monster such as this.

The woman narrowed her eyes and

curled her lips into a menacing smile. Chills bolted through Valeria's body. "So, this is the powerful demigod Daughter of Nike everyone keeps talking about," she boomed, her voice deep and raspy. "Not so strong now, it seems. She cannot even defeat Hades's minions of death. Still, she will be most delicious to the Mother of Monsters; it has been a long time since she has tasted the flesh of a demigod."

Valeria gulped. She needed to bide as much time as she could, build up her strength, and use her powers against this beast without burning herself up. "Hey, the Mother of Monsters, huh? This should be interesting. Do I at least get to meet her before, uh, she tastes my flesh? Or were you planning on killing me first? I'll probably be tastier the fresher I am, so you should wait to kill me until after I meet her."

Greg gawked at Valeria. "What the hell are you doing?"

The woman chuckled, squishing the last

of the corpses. "Ha-ha. Demigods are funny. This one is no exception. Echidna, the Mother of Monsters, wife of the dreaded Typhon, and mother of Orthrus and many others, stands before funny demigod now. Zeus himself sent the Mother of Monsters to kill you. She does not like Zeus, but who could say no to treats as tasty as a demigod and her little human friend? It has been many years since she was able to eat so well."

Valeria narrowed her eyes. This wasn't the first time she'd heard about Zeus today. He was another god she knew from Greek mythology, although all she could remember about him was he slept with just about everything that walked. Valeria was pretty sure he had some big bad lightning bolt that helped him rule the skies or something like that also. Why had he sent Echidna to kill her? Was that the gods' plan all along, and why Nike had needed to protect her? Why Hades had sent his zombies after her?

Not only that, but what did Greg have to do with all this? Why had the gods allowed him to live when they'd killed everyone else in town other than her, only to let Echidna eat him in the end?

At this point, it probably didn't matter. For however long this monster would talk, Valeria needed to stall. "Oh man, it all makes sense now. I mean, that Orthrus is your son—the resemblance is *uncanny*. Anyway, I'm so sorry about killing him and all. I hope there's no hard feelings! He just ate my dad and was gonna kill me, you know. I'm sure other than that he was a very agreeable dog."

"Silly demigod will find Echidna to be much fiercer than her two-headed son," Echidna said, squeezing Greg in her hand. He writhed and screamed.

Valeria rushed forward. "Stop! You're hurting him!"

Echidna laughed. "Small demigod does

not like when the Mother of Monsters pinches her friend's insides?"

"No, I don't," Valeria said, brandishing the knife. "Let him go. It's me you want."

"Val, no . . ." Greg whimpered.

The monster paused. "Daughter of Nike is correct," she said, and tossed Greg to the side. He bounced off the road a few times and crashed into a wrecked car, then lay still.

Valeria gasped and bolted toward him, but Echidna slammed her serpent tail onto the road. The impact sent Valeria flying backward along with chunks of asphalt. She slammed back-first into the ground and lost hold of the dagger. Sharp pains shot through her body, the wind knocked out of her.

Echidna slithered to Valeria, plucked her up by her now-free arm, and dangled her at eye level. "See how easily the Mother of Monsters made demigod a snack? Now all she must do is cook her. Perhaps she will eat her with the

Shield of Nike. That will make her nice and crunchy. Ha-ha!"

Echidna held her torch under Valeria's feet, heat and smoke spiraling around her, invading her nose and mouth. Valeria hacked, her chest on fire. She'd run out of time. Her strength wasn't back at all, and now the Mother of Monsters was about to eat her, then Greg too.

I've failed, she thought, hanging her head. *This is the end.*

You will only fail if you give up now, my child, said Nike in Valeria's mind. *If you try, perhaps you have enough power to slay Echidna.*

Valeria closed her eyes. *But what happens if I use too much power and die, and Echidna eats us anyway? What then? We'll both be dead. All of this will have been for nothing.*

That is a risk all must take, Nike replied. *Do you think a single hero who has ever been born knows for certain if they will survive their most perilous quest? Do you think any mortal knows for a fact whether or not they will live to see another day? No one ever knows anything for sure, not even the gods. There are many different outcomes to any given situation. But the reason anyone keeps on living is because they persevere. Through perseverance, they at least have a chance.*

Valeria opened her eyes and stared down at the scorching flames licking below her feet. *Please, Valeria*, Nike continued. *Persevere. You could die trying, yes. But what if you live?*

"Demigod is not cooking fast enough," Echidna said. "The Mother of Monsters will start her on fire. That should do the trick."

Valeria glanced over at Greg still lying motionless on the side of the road. Nike was right. She could die fighting Echidna. But if she lived, she could save her best friend's life.

At the thought of a chance to save him, even a slim one, a familiar sense of purpose flooded her body. Her muscles ignited with power. She clenched her jaw, swung herself

toward Echidna's face and, using the momentum, kicked the monster as hard as she could in one glowing red eye.

The Mother of Monsters shrieked, throwing her hands in the air. Valeria and the torch went flying. The torch hit a nearby truck. Within moments the vehicle burst into flames, illuminating the surrounding area with golden light. Meanwhile, Valeria used the shield as a barrier between herself and the ground as she landed, hoping it would cushion her fall.

When she tumbled into the road, her arm, shoulder, and knees erupted with pain, but she couldn't let that stop her. She had to keep going. She pulled herself to her feet, seized the knife she'd dropped earlier, and swung around to face the monster.

Echidna wailed and raised her tail, then brought it down at Valeria full-force. Valeria somersaulted to the side. The tail collided with the street, sending chunks of asphalt soaring.

Valeria held up the shield to block debris from hitting her.

"Stupid demigod!" Echidna yelled, covering her injured eye with one hand. "The Mother of Monsters will play these silly games, but she will make them long and horrible for her opponent!"

Valeria racked her brain for an idea. How in the world could she kill a thirty-foot-tall snake-lady?

The monster brought her tail down on Valeria's other side. Valeria stumbled backward. Rubble rained on her head. "Ha-ha! Echidna can do this all night! But Daughter of Nike will run out of stamina sooner or later!"

Valeria knit her brow; she had an idea now. She prayed to whatever god on her side it would work, then, although her chest burned, focused her speed and bolted straight for the Mother of Monsters.

Everything around her blurred. She ran

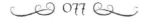

up Echidna's body. Within half a second, she reached the monster's shoulder. Echidna shouted, swatting at Valeria, trying to knock her off. She used her speed to dodge the attacks.

Valeria gripped the dagger tight. She brought her arm back and rammed the blade through Echidna's throat.

Green fluid oozed from the wound, but Valeria didn't stop there. She tore the weapon through the monster's neck. Echidna let out a gurgling scream and flailed her hands. One slap sent Valeria flying. As she hit the street, something in her chest cracked. Intense pain shot along every inch of her body. She groaned, her vision fading between red and black.

Echidna ripped the dagger from her neck and tossed it behind her. A liquid similar to the one oozing from her throat filled her mouth and trickled from her lips.

Valeria's breaths were cut short by sharp pains in her chest. The pains weren't anything like the burning sensation she experienced when she overexerted her powers, though: she guessed she had some broken ribs.

Her whole body ached and stung. She was surely covered in bruises and cuts. But she still held out hope and pulled herself to her feet; Echidna wouldn't last forever with the kind of damage Valeria had inflicted. She just needed to fight until the Mother of Monsters couldn't any longer.

The monster slithered toward Valeria and hissed, "Prepare to die, Daughter of Nike."

"Try me, you ugly-ass overgrown snake," Valeria spat, raising the shield.

Echidna roared and swung her serpent tail at Valeria. It rammed into the shield, and Valeria stumbled backward. The monster pulled her tail back, surely preparing to bring it down again. Before she could, Valeria channeled her speed and darted to the side.

Before Echidna could attack again, Valeria

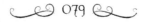

removed the shield from her arm. With one hand she held it above her head. Her chest burned, her ribs screaming, but she concentrated her strength. Using what she was sure was the last of her power, she gathered as much momentum as she could and chucked the shield at the monster's neck.

The shield spun toward Echidna like a frisbee. Its orange-gold metal sliced through the last of her throat, her glowing red eyes going wide. Her head jerked all the way back. Valeria thought it might fall off entirely, but it dangled from a thin piece of leathery skin and a couple of tendons dripping with green fluid, more of which spilled from the monster's stump.

Echidna swayed back and forth a few times, then crashed into the road. The impact shook the ground. For a few moments, Valeria waited for the monster to make a move. But she only lay in the street, perfectly still.

Relief washed through Valeria. She'd done

it; she'd killed the Mother of Monsters. Now she could finally reunite with her friend.

She turned toward Greg to run to him, but a wave of dizziness struck her. She trembled. Beads of sweat popped up all over her skin. She felt as though she were overheating from the inside. *This is it*, she thought. *I overused my powers, and now I'm dead. At least I gave Greg a chance. Please, Greg, wake up and get away from here.*

Beside Valeria, blinding light flashed and Nike appeared. She opened her arms to her daughter. "You will live to see another day."

Valeria's knees buckled. She fell over and slipped into unconsciousness.

CHAPTER EIGHT
FUTURE

When Valeria gained consciousness next, she felt rejuvenated, as if her body had been made new. Pain no longer shot along her ribs, nor did her chest burn, and surprisingly, after all she'd been through, she didn't sting or ache a bit. She smiled and opened her eyes, then yawned and stretched, taking in her surroundings.

She lay in the street she'd fought Echidna in the night before. The sun rose at a snail's pace above the horizon, although still blocked somewhat by gray clouds. On one side of her, Nike, who now had her shield back, knelt watching her, as did a handsome man with a quiver of golden arrows slung over his shoulder and a bow in hand. The man's eyes were bright green, his hair a curly strawberry-blond. He wore white robes, and rays of light shone off his tanned body. Valeria guessed he was another one of the gods.

"Good morning," he said, his voice smooth and melodious.

On Valeria's other side, Greg sat watching her too. To her surprise, he appeared uninjured after everything he'd been through, and she hoped there wasn't any damage done to him that she couldn't see.

She sat up and faced him, her heart racing. He gave her a smile. "It's good to see you again," he said.

Valeria's eyes filled with tears. "You too."

"C'mere," Greg said, and enveloped her in a hug. He smelled the same as he always did: like a cool forest breeze. "When I woke up, Echidna was dead, and that guy"—he gestured toward the man in white next to Nike—"had healed me. I asked him if you were okay, and he said he'd healed you, too, because you'd gotten hurt killing Echidna. I asked how you did it, and he told me the whole story. So badass."

Valeria squeezed him tight. "Thank you. But to be honest, I wouldn't have had the willpower to kill her if there weren't a chance to save you in the process."

Greg pulled out of the hug and cupped her cheek with his palm. "After the arrow hit me and I passed out, the next thing I remember was waking up and learning what was going on—a couple of the gods themselves explained it. They told me all my family . . ." His eyes grew watery, and he choked back a sob. "They told me my family was dead. My parents, my sisters . . . everyone. They said my friends were dead too. I wanted to know why I was still alive. Like, why me, you know? I didn't have the will to keep on living after that. I wanted to die too. But then they told me you were still out there, that you were looking for me, and I knew I had to hold on, even when they handed me off to Echidna. If there was a chance to be with you again, then I still had a reason to be here, even if everyone else was gone."

"I love you, Greg," Valeria said. "I'm in love with you. I think I have been for a long time."

"I love you too, Val," Greg said, and kissed her. When their lips touched, warm tingles fluttered through her body. She'd kissed boys before, but kissing Greg was different. She couldn't help but feel that right here, right now, was exactly where she'd always been meant to be. They pulled out of the kiss. He gave her a crooked grin.

The handsome man next to Nike cleared his throat, and Valeria and Greg turned to face him. He climbed to his feet. Standing, he was as tall as Nike. "Allow me to introduce myself. I am Apollo, God of Sunlight, Healing, Archery,

Music, Art, Oracles, and Poetry."

"Well, that's a mouthful," Valeria re-marked.

Apollo opened his arms in a welcoming gesture. "I was sent not only to heal you and your friend, Daughter of Nike, but also to congratulate you for excelling in all of the tests Zeus, King of the Gods, made for you. On his behalf I'd like to welcome you both to live on New Mount Olympus alongside many of the gods. There, your friend will act as a servant in the palace, while you will train to become one of the first Warriors of the Gods."

Valeria's jaw dropped. She looked to Nike, but the goddess wouldn't meet her eyes. She only gazed down at the ground as if in guilt.

Everything Valeria had gone through, the confusion, the trauma, the fights—it had *all* been one giant test. Not just Orthrus, but the zombies and Echidna too . . .

Nike had known it all along.

"What do you mean, a Warrior of the Gods?" Valeria asked.

"You know about all that has happened, do you not?" Apollo replied. "We, the Greek gods, are real. Humanity stopped worshipping us, and we'd finally had enough, so we destroyed the modern world as you know it. We plan to take back the worship we deserve. Zeus directed the storms and lightning, my twin sister Artemis and I sent the arrows, Poseidon made the earthquakes, and Hades brought the corpses back to life. Not only that, but you are a demigod child-of-Nike, and the gifts of strength and speed were bestowed upon you at birth." Valeria gave a slow nod. "Oh, good. I thought you knew the details, but I needed to make sure. In that case, I will make this quick. As a Warrior of the Gods, you will not only live in luxury on New Mount Olympus, but you will also have the pleasure of ensuring that humanity is not led astray again. You will make them worship us, and if any decide to revolt, you will take care of them."

"Take care of them?"

"Why, you will kill them, of course. There is no better way to deal with insubordination."

Valeria couldn't believe what she was hearing. "Wouldn't it be better if people made the choice to worship you? Wouldn't that mean more?"

Apollo sneered. "We already gave humanity a choice, and they abandoned us. To rule again, we must obliterate 'choice.' We will never allow something so silly as free will to stand in our way again."

Valeria stood and balled her fists. "No."

"No?" Apollo asked, raising an eyebrow.

"You heard me. No. Greg isn't going to be your little servant. And I won't make people worship you. I won't be a Warrior of the Gods."

"And why not?"

"You destroyed the world just because

people don't believe in you anymore. You killed everyone in my town, including my father. You don't deserve praise or prayers. You deserve to fade away."

"Well, there's no need to be disrespectful," Apollo replied. "We thought allowing your friend to be a servant in the palace would sweeten the deal. Are you certain?"

Greg climbed to his feet and took Valeria's hand. She laced her fingers with his. "You heard me. No means no; end of discussion. Neither of us will work for you."

Apollo shrugged. "Very well. If you will not come to New Mount Olympus, I was instructed to kill you. So now you must die."

Valeria and Greg locked eyes, and Greg squeezed her hand. Neither of them had to say anything; they knew what the other was thinking. If they died now, they'd die together, and at least then the gods couldn't use either of them to do their bidding.

"There will be no deaths today," Nike piped up, striding in front of Apollo to block him from Valeria and Greg. "Let them go. They have suffered enough."

Apollo frowned. "You dare to challenge an Olympian? To challenge Zeus's ruling? Do not be foolish, Nike. You may be one of Zeus's favorites, but this is a crime he will throw even you into Tartarus for."

Nike raised her shield. There was a flash of light in her free hand, and the same orange-gold dagger she'd allowed Valeria to use appeared in her palm. Apollo pulled an arrow from the quiver on his back and readied his bow. "You two, leave now," Nike said. "I will keep you safe for as long as I can."

Valeria and Greg didn't wait to see what would happen next. Hand in hand they ran away from the scene, past the crushed zombies, past Echidna's corpse, past the fallen buildings, back to Greg's car. Once the pair reached the vehicle, Valeria gave Greg the keys. He started the engine. Behind them, golden light blasted through the sky. The sounds of arrows *whoosh*ing and metal clashing echoed across the debris.

The pair sped out of town. Where they would go, Valeria couldn't be sure. She had no idea what would happen next. How would they survive this hellish landscape? What monsters awaited them now? Would the gods come after them? Not only that, but would Nike be okay? Valeria hadn't known her for very long, but the goddess was her mother and had guided and protected her, and had even protected her father. It was hard not to care.

For now, Valeria decided she wouldn't worry about any of those things. She and Greg were together again, and they were in love. They'd find a way to persevere.

* ⁓ * ⁓ * ⁓

Two years later . . .

Fall, Year 2 AS

Apollo stayed several feet behind Artemis as the pair dashed through the thick forest between their two cities. A quiver of golden arrows was slung over his shoulder, bow in hand, the grass beneath his bare feet cool and dewy.

The sun had not risen yet, so his sister, as a goddess of the moon, remained ahead of him. But as soon as the sun came up, he would be the unstoppable one. For now, however, he was content with staying in Artemis's shadow, her frizzy red curls flying behind her.

For the last few hours, the twins had been hunting a band of mortals who had not only betrayed the gods and gone to live on their own outside the cities, but who had also managed to cast some sort of cloaking spell so they could not be discovered easily. The insolent fools! Once Apollo and Artemis found the mortals, they planned to show no mercy.

A while longer into their search, the sun crept above the horizon. Bursts of invigorating power coursed through Apollo's veins. He sped past Artemis and, for a few moments, stayed ahead of her. That is, until a sharp pain rushed through his head.

He cried out, collapsing in the grass as more pains came and went. It felt as though someone were stabbing his skull over and over.

"Brother, what ails you?" Artemis cried, kneeling next to him and resting a hand on his back.

The last time he had experienced this kind of pain, he had been given a vision of the future. "A p-prophecy is c-coming," he said, and images flashed before his eyes.

He saw Zeus holding Planet Earth in his burly hands, then forests with monsters lurking at every corner. He saw the blood of a demigod spilling over debris, and the shadows of two mortals from the Before Time rising from death. He saw a stormy black sky illuminated with peridot-green lightning bolts. The two mortals flew on the backs of pegasi, a furious army behind them, toward New Mount Olympus.

What could this mean for the gods?

He gasped and came to. Artemis still knelt beside him. As though possessed by an evil force, he looked up at her and relayed in his own words the future events he had witnessed. "*When the world is taken back, and monsters rule the trees, blood of a demigod will spill. Two mortals will rise, two from the Before, reborn from sacrifice. And when the sky is black and green, and the heavens cry, they will lead a war. A war on the gods.*"

Artemis helped Apollo to his feet. "We must tell Zeus and the other Olympians what you have seen."

Read more about the gods, monsters, and heroes of this world in the first installment of the War on the Gods Trilogy, *The Helm of Darkness*, where Apollo's prophecy finally comes to fruition . . .

Get *The Helm of Darkness* on Amazon
NOW!

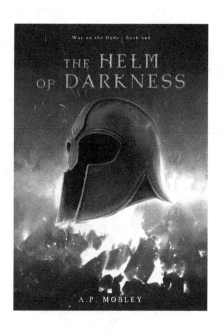

A. P. Mobley is a young-adult fantasy author with an undying love for Greek mythology and epic, magical tales. She grew up in Wyoming and currently lives there, working part-time as a substitute teacher and studying to earn her degree in English. She considers herself a huge nerd, loves chocolate a little too much, and can be found snuggling with one of her pets into late hours of the night.

Follow her on Twitter and Instagram: @author_apmobley.

If you liked *The Shield of Nike*, make sure to leave it a review on Amazon and Goodreads! Reviews help authors, and if you'd like to see more stories from A. P. Mobley, make sure to review her works.

CPSIA information can be obtained
at www.ICGtesting.com
Printed in the USA
LVHW020427061220
673478LV00030B/560

9 781732 093720